T0057557

BY FIRE

BY FIRE
Writings on the Arab Spring

TAHAR BEN JELLOUN

Translated from the French
and with an introduction by Rita S. Nezami

CURBSTONE BOOKS

NORTHWESTERN UNIVERSITY PRESS

EVANSTON, ILLINOIS

Curbstone Books
Northwestern University Press
www.nupress.northwestern.edu

Printed in the United States of America

10   9   8   7   6   5   4   3   2   1

Library of Congress Cataloging-in-Publication Data
Names: Ben Jelloun, Tahar, 1944– author. | Nezami, Rita S., translator, writer of introduction. | Ben Jelloun, Tahar, 1944– Par le feu. Translation of: | Ben Jelloun, Tahar, 1944– L'Etincelle. Abridgement of (work): | Ben Jelloun, Tahar, 1944– L'Etincelle. Translation of:
Title: By fire : writings on the Arab Spring / Tahar Ben Jelloun ; translated from the French and with an introduction by Rita S. Nezami.
Description: Evanston, Illinois : Curbstone Books/Northwestern University Press, 2016. | "This book contains [Rita S. Nezami's] translations of By fire and sections related to the Tunisian conflict from The spark . . . Also included is [a] translation of a brief reflection on the new Tunisian Constitution by Ben Jelloun." | "Par le feu was originally published in French by Gallimard in 2011, (c) Editions Gallimard 2011 . . . L'etincelle was originally published in French by Gallimard in 2011, (c) Editions Gallimard."
Identifiers: LCCN 2016001924| ISBN 9780810133396 (pbk. : alk. paper) | ISBN 9780810133402 (e-book)
Subjects: LCSH: Bouazizi, Mohamed, 1984–2011—Fiction. | Protest movements—Tunisia—History—21st century—Fiction. | Tunisia—History—Demonstrations, 2010– | Tunisia—Politics and government—2011-
Classification: LCC PQ3989.2.J4 A2 2016 | DDC 843.914—dc23
LC record available at http://lccn.loc.gov/2016001924

"Fire destroys that which feeds it."
—SIMONE WEIL

Albert Camus asked, "What is a rebel?"
and answering his own question, he said:
"A man who says no." It is at this point,
when fear is gone, that whole nations say no."
—PETER BEAUMONT, "HOW DICTATORS FALL"

Contents

Translator's Acknowledgments

I would like to thank Jeffrey Green for his edits and suggestions on the book's introduction; Marilyn Zucker, Peter Khost, and Astrid Wimmer for reading my translation of *Par le feu*; Franck Dalmas for his help with aspects of *L'étincelle*'s translation. Above all, I wish to express my gratitude to my publisher-father, the late Ruhul Amin Nezami, for inspiring me.

Translator's Introduction

Browsing in a Paris bookshop in the summer of 2011, I picked up two books by Moroccan writer Tahar Ben Jelloun, the novella *Par le feu* (*By Fire*) and the nonfiction *L'étincelle* (*The Spark*)—both works about the Arab Spring. A juggernaut of revolts against authoritarian regimes, the Arab Spring began the previous winter with uprisings throughout several countries in North Africa and the Middle East. At hand, the experts said, may be an era of fundamental political reform throughout the region. Journalists and political analysts were virtually unanimous that the Arab world was convulsively re-creating itself while we watched. Some North African and Middle Eastern countries would be changed in some way by the firestorm. Ben Jelloun published the two books with Gallimard in 2011 at the height of the protests.

The *New Yorker* published my translation of *By Fire* in September 2013, which gave many American readers the first opportunity to learn about Mohamed Bouazizi, the young Tunisian man who is often credited with triggering the Arab Spring. *By Fire* makes it possible for American and European Anglophone readers to gain insights into the personal life of a tormented and economically marginalized man. Certainly, the international media covered the demonstrations from Tunis to Cairo by showing furious demonstrators clashing with the police, but often a reporter's voice-over gave viewers a superficial update on the current state of revolts and negotiations before quickly moving on to the next story. The media could not show the experiences of individuals who finally had enough of oppression and deprivation. Though the cameras *did* zoom onto individual faces and microphones *did* capture the shouting and tumult, journalists could not reveal the people's subjective experience of intense despair and frustration. Perhaps even the most meticulous historical writing cannot always capture the experience and meaning of a mortar round that turns bedrooms into glass shards and rubble. "Showing" and not "telling" is easier for the novelist: in the literary imagination, one can more easily enter a life, a mind, a space, and a specific moment and show what one finds there. Writers like Ben Jelloun use the full range of their literary and imaginative powers to represent the human condition that can evade chronological or historical narratives. In *By Fire*, he critically reveals the consequences of tyranny and repression through the eyes and emotions of one street vendor in the vast Arab world. *The Spark*, on the other hand, reports and objectively analyzes this moment in history and focuses on various historical figures, including Mohamed Bouazizi. *The Spark* also represents an irreverent and fearless snapshot of dictatorship and the politics of the Arab Spring as it stood in 2011.

THIS BOOK CONTAINS my translations of *By Fire* and sections related to the Tunisian conflict from *The Spark*. These selections are vital for a serious reading of the novella and will enrich the experiences of first-time and veteran readers of Ben Jelloun. *The Spark* also provides a rich background against which to read *By Fire*. Also included is my translation of a brief reflection on the new Tunisian Constitution by Ben Jelloun. My task in this introduction is to offer some comments that may open the story for readers and help them enter it with confidence.

The Arab Spring: Essential Backstory

By Fire has its roots in mid-1950s Tunisian politics. Considering how the autonomous Tunisia was born reveals a lot about how Mohamed Bouazizi reached his soul-wrenching impasse in a small Tunisian town, Sidi Bouzid, more than a half century later. Zine al-Abidine Ben Ali came to power in Tunisia because electoral institutions never found footing as the weary French colonial rulers moved toward handing power over to the Tunisians. In 1957, for the first time the people elected a constituent assembly, which declared Habib Bourguiba as president. Bourguiba then ruled—and was even granted the title of president-for-life by a constitutional amendment in 1975—until Ben Ali ousted him in 1987. Bourguiba had long been at the forefront of the Tunisian independence movement and spent years in French prisons for his beliefs. Leader of the Neo-Destour Party, Bourguiba found widespread support among the people, but he was no democrat, and many called him a dictator once he came to power. However, he was committed to a secular state and went so far as to criticize what he regarded as the negative effects of Ramadan on the Tunisian economy. To the dismay of other Arab leaders, he maintained good relations with the West and did not mince words about his East-West orientation: "Basically and profoundly, we are with the West," he said in 1957 as Tunisia was coming together as an independent state. Perhaps this was true in terms of trade and secularism, but it was not in terms of political power, and it was precisely this kind of thinking about how and where power should reside that set the stage for Tunisia's future police-state ("Tunisia: Neighbor's Duty" 1957). Bourguiba esteemed Western values while, at the same time, thinking that such values, especially democracy, were not appropriate for Tunisia. "The state and its existence are essential before everything else," he said in 1958. "All this preoccupation with liberty is not serious" ("Tunisia: No Time for Democracy" 1958).

This rhetoric betrayed the strength of authoritarianism that would come to dominate Tunisian life and eventually catch people like Bouazizi in its maw. Bourguiba loathed colonialism, but he was convinced that democracy should not be its successor. In the September 29, 1958, issue of *Time* magazine, Bourguiba spelled out his thinking about the relationship between political liberty and nation-building: "At the moment of a revolution there is no question of setting up a democracy like that in America. If they accuse me of dictatorship, I accept. I am creating a nation. Liberty must be suppressed until the end of the war in Algeria—until the nation becomes homogeneous" ("Tunisia: No Time for Democracy" 1958).

The combination of dictatorships and the absence of the rule of law ended badly. When the French left, there was a vacuum that the Neo-Destour Party and Bourguiba's authoritarianism filled. Thirty years later, when Bourguiba grew old and feeble, there was, again, a vacuum, and Ben Ali, Bourguiba's prime minister, was more than ready to fill it. In 1987, claiming Bourguiba was too ill and elderly to run the country, Ben Ali removed the president from power and named himself his successor.

In her comparative work on postcolonial North African political systems, *Human Rights and Reform: Changing the Face of North African Politics*, Susan Waltz describes the disappointment of those who hoped the region would include reforms that vested political power in the people. Instead, the postcolonial state maintained control by defaulting to repression and civil-rights abuses (Waltz 1995). Glacier-size forces drive the fortunes of the anonymous masses, and it is Bourguiba's legacy that made possible his succession by a man preoccupied with power, control, and personal wealth, and which, many years later, cost Mohamed Bouazizi his ability to support his family without selling out.

For twenty-three years, the Ben Ali regime stayed in power by clamping down on opposition, controlling the media, and liberally detaining and torturing citizens it suspected of being regime opponents. Omar Mestiri, secretary-general for the National Council for Freedom in Tunisia, said, "Torture occurs in the very rooms where the Universal Declaration of Human Rights is hanging on the wall. Any tortured person can attest to that" ("Tunisia Country Profile" 2007). The people on the street knew the judiciary was rigged and that regulations crafted by Ben Ali funneled vast wealth to his clan. Especially infuriated were the educated unemployed who had played by the rules, gone to school, studied diligently, and now could not feed their families. In January 2011, less than a month after Bouazizi's death, the BBC reported that this huge bloc of talented and well-educated but unemployed young people was overcome by frustration with lack of freedoms, the excesses of the ruling class, and anger at police brutality. "It's all come together," the BBC wrote, "to spark an unstoppable wave of public anger" ("Q&A: Tunisia Crisis" 2011).

Some familiarity with what started the Arab Spring may enrich readers' experience of Ben Jelloun's fiction and nonfiction. A reliable narrative of what exactly happened in Sidi Bouzid, before Mohamed Bouazizi set himself ablaze in December 2010, remains elusive, but the main features are clear. A fruit and vegetable seller, Bouazizi was exasperated by his trouble with the municipal government, which looked the other way when police harassed street sellers, demanded they pay bribes, and whimsically imposed fines for missing permits, even if permits were not required. "Mohamed was in trouble because agents from the council were asking for bribes every time he was buying and selling his vegetables," said his sister Samia ("Memories of a Tunisian Martyr" 2011). The police and inspectors routinely roughed up street vendors and brazenly helped themselves to the men's wares. Bouazizi was the sole supporter of his widowed mother and siblings, and the local culture of petty bribery and harassment stifled his ability to feed his family.

December 17, 2010, turned lethal when Bouazizi got into a row with municipal inspector Fedia Hamdi, who allegedly slapped and spat on him while her colleagues beat him. Although this incident of a woman culturally emasculating an Arab man is central to the popular narrative of "Bouazizi as martyr," readers should be aware that Hamdi denied using physical violence, that the Bouazizi family dropped charges against her, and that she was exonerated after the revolution ("Tunisia Revolt" 2011). The police claimed they confiscated his fruit cart and scales because Bouazizi lacked a vendor's permit and was selling from what may have been a restricted area near government buildings. Hamdi stated at the trial that Bouazizi subsequently went into a rage. Sources agree that, publicly humiliated, Bouazizi first made his way to the municipal building, where authorities refused to return his fruit cart, and, instead, beat him. The governor's office staff further ignored his demand to appeal his case. Then, desperate and perhaps irrational, Bouazizi, standing at the governor's high gate, in the midst of traffic, cried out, "How do you expect me to make a living?" (Simon

2011). Bouazizi then doused himself with fuel and self-immolated in public.

The spectacle of Bouazizi's public self-immolation is widely regarded as having ignited the first revolts in Tunisia. Yet, his was not a cry to bring down the twenty-three-year-old regime of Ben Ali, a narrative protestors quickly took up. "Ah, he was protesting the oppressive and morally corroded state!" cried people who leveraged Mohamed's suicide for political ends by imposing on him the martyr's role rather than considering that he may have simply been a man at the end of his rope. His was probably the cry of a man left with no good choices about making a living in the barren and dusty outpost of Sidi Bouzid, a town of only thirty-six thousand people near the center of Tunisia. Sidi Bouzid's poor live in boxlike structures that can scarcely be called houses. It was with the bureaucracy and corruption of this obscure town that Bouazizi had problems. He could not endure the daily struggle and pressure to feed his family and remain beholden to the local government's petty tyrannies. In this, the municipal corruption that drove Bouazizi to destroy himself in a fit of long-repressed fury reflected the ethically fetid national government of Ben Ali. Sidi Bouzid is real; it is on the map; it is where Bouazizi killed himself. But, as Ben Jelloun writes fiction, not history, he asks that we don't enforce Sidi Bouzid as the setting of *By Fire*. He leaves it for readers to think through the relationship between the historical and the literary, between the real and the imagined place in *By Fire*.

BEN JELLOUN'S *BY FIRE* asks that we not conflate Sidi Bouzid or Mohamed Bouazizi with the setting of his fiction. The work does not pretend to be a literary reading of what happened to Bouazizi that December day. Instead, Ben Jelloun lets the story float in a Middle Eastern–like space. He never names the town, the country, its president, its currency, or anything that locks the narrative into particulars. Further, Mohamed Bouazizi's surname never appears in *By Fire*—he remains, simply, "Mohamed." (The actual date of Bouazizi's death is an exception that surfaces near the end of the novella.) Despite the historical material's importance, the story is freestanding: in many ways, it can be read without knowing any more than what is on the page. Readers can decide whether they experience the story differently if and when the historical record informs their reading. By allowing Ben Jelloun to take us into the world of *By Fire*'s Mohamed, we make the same agreement we make with any artist: we consent to be led into a sphere of his creation wherein we can see with greater subtlety and sensitivity the life and death of a poor street vendor.

The story initially appears to be a simple literary re-telling of what happened in a small town in Tunisia during a couple of months in 2010 and 2011. However, that reading, though understandable, is mistaken. *By Fire* stands alone as a short work of literature; it is art. The protagonist in *By Fire* is not necessarily the Mohamed Bouazizi of history. Ben Jelloun's protagonist is not contingent on the historical. The historical figure's doubling makes no difference to the vitality and originality of the story *as art*.

Literature's and history's ends are different. Ben Jelloun wrote a story, so, given that the historical record and the story's plot track each other, the question becomes, Why is the story necessary? Perhaps Ben Jelloun hoped to accomplish *as a literary artist* what he felt lay beyond the historian's boundaries. We have two Mohameds, and they must both remain vital as readers think about Ben Jelloun's story *and* about the real-life fruit vendor. In the space between the historical Bouazizi and his protagonist, Ben Jelloun imaginatively enters *his* Mohamed's consciousness, and readers benefit from the insights he discovers in the process.

Long before Ben Jelloun wrote *Par le feu*, Milan Kundera captured what serious writers do. "I invent stories," Kundera told Philip Roth, "confront one with another, and by this means I ask questions. The stupidity of people comes from having an answer for everything. The wisdom of the novel comes from having a question for everything. . . . The novelist teaches the reader to comprehend the world as a question. There is wisdom and tolerance in that attitude" (Kundera and Heim 1981, 237). Ben Jelloun's project is of a piece with Kundera's: to continuously interrogate anxiety, fear, anger, and loss, and thereby refine readers' perceptions of a messy and complex reality. *By Fire* is not an inquiry into Tunisian politics. It is an imaginative exploration of *one man's* experience at a specific moment. It asks questions. It probes, disturbs, disrupts.

It is in the geography between Mohamed Bouazizi's real life and Ben Jelloun's creation of his double where readers are invited to explore Mohamed's desperation, his hopelessness, how he wants to care for his family, and his path toward suicide. These personal elements are perhaps harder to make available through historical inquiry. Through fiction, Ben Jelloun takes up these questions when he imagines Mohamed's despair because the police confiscate his cart. The author implicates power and its corruption in police harassment and unresponsive municipal officials. He also maps

Mohamed's trajectory toward self-destruction by correlating it with unrelenting and escalating pressure and frustration and, ultimately, fatal desperation about how he could possibly be defeated by the state in caring for his family. Ben Jelloun offers us the chance to walk *with* this character through the streets of Mohamed's small town as he encounters corruption and violence. The author renders the tortured complexities of political legitimacy and the relationship between the individual and the state by bringing them to bear on a street vendor and his rickety fruit cart. By imagining his way into Mohamed's life, Ben Jelloun represents how the state's reckless use of power ruined a man. The question of why the historical Bouazizi chooses death, and such a painful one, mocks itself because the only source of an answer is unreachable. The question became unanswerable the moment he touched the flame to his clothes. He did not and could not articulate his thinking before dying, so only the question survives. By rendering the incident as a story, Ben Jelloun preserves the question while refusing a facile answer. In fact, any answer would diminish the question's integrity by tainting it with answers' certainty. Ben Jelloun gives us in *By Fire* an intimate look at Mohamed's last days and then steps away, allowing for question-asking.

By Fire (Par le feu)

By Fire is the first work of fiction on the Arab Spring. Ben Jelloun wrote this novella within a few months; I understood why there was such urgency. The spectacle of the Arab Spring spread worldwide *as it happened*. Every time a protester on Tahrir Square screamed, there was not a corner of the world where it could not be heard. News of Bouazizi's self-immolation went viral in moments, and the event demanded immediate attention, coverage, and contemplation. Ben Jelloun was so moved that he decided to fictionalize Bouazizi's last days. "I saw him on his bed like a white mummy and thought to myself: 'This man had a life, a youth, a failed love affair, disappointments.' I wanted to return his humanity to him," Ben Jelloun told *Deutsche Welle* (Thomas 2011). To return dignity and humanity to the young man, Ben Jelloun's ethical responsibility led him to create Bouazizi's double.

So why write a story that looks so much like the historical event itself? Why call his protagonist Mohamed? Is it because fiction can do what nonfiction often cannot, namely, reach readers at a deeper level and appeal more to their emotions? In fiction, the historical Bouazizi's face no longer remains just another anonymous face in the crowd. Instead, he becomes a multidimensional character: a son, a brother, a lover, and a marginal subject who takes a rad-ically self-destructive action. Ben Jelloun wanted to cap-ture this critical moment in the life of an individual to show what kind of suffering *can* lead to suicide.

In September 2013, Ben Jelloun shared some of his thoughts about *By Fire* with Deborah Treisman, fiction editor of the *New Yorker* in "This Week in Fiction: Tahar Ben Jelloun":

> I had written articles and an essay attempting to explain the roots of this "Spring." But those piec-es were missing a literary perspective, a fictional perspective that could depart from the raw facts. I needed to express, as a novelist, what I, as an observer and a citizen, was thinking. I'm sure that literature—fiction—has the ability to reach readers more effectively than any television news report. I focused on Mohamed's story, I closed my eyes, I saw it, and I wrote it. Beyond the specific situation in Tunisia, Mohamed Bouazizi became a valuable symbol for all cultures and all countries in pursuit of dignity. (Treisman 2013)

Ben Jelloun spoke directly to the problem of the tension between the novelist and the historian: "I was faithful to the profound meaning of Mohamed Bouazizi's terrible act. But I also did my job as a novelist. I imagined his circle, his behavior, his actions. I kept it universal even as I was very tied to the specifics. I think that many people reading this story will recognize themselves in this character or identify with him" (Treisman 2013). *By Fire* depicts universal themes. Reading *By Fire* along with *The Spark* will help readers understand and even identify with Mohamed's character based on Bouazizi's real life. *The Spark* helps us understand the historical figure's experience in a corrupt, dictatorial regime.

The Spark (L'étincelle)

The chapters selected from *The Spark* focus on former Tunisian president Zine al-Abidine Ben Ali's corrupt regime; how he deposed President Habib Bourguiba, an educated and a visionary man, in 1987; and Mohamed Bouazizi's difficult life and death. Unlike *By Fire*, which takes us into Mohamed's head, *The Spark* begins by taking the reader into the heads of Egypt's Hosni Mubarak and Tunisia's Ben Ali after both flee like thieves from their countries. It finally dawns on the two dictators that they have lost their grip on power in 2011, after the revolts in Tunisia and Egypt. Using light mockery and humor,

Ben Jelloun portrays the two exiled dictators: "While Mubarak has a headache, what is Ben Ali, the Tunisian, who fled from his country on January 14, doing?... What does he do with his days? He watches television. He just lies around. He too [like Mubarak] doesn't feel like coloring his hair. He is depressed. He lives in a gilded prison [Saudi Arabia]." Throughout the book Ben Jelloun condemns the dictators' brutality, unmasks their greed, corruption, and total indifference toward their people. After Bouazizi's brutal suicide, writes Ben Jelloun in *The Spark*, "with calm and dignity, Tunisians rose as one. It was the police who were violent; their brutality left several dozen dead and hundreds of others wounded. Submissive for twenty-three years to a quiet dictatorship, the people succeeded in bringing down Ben Ali, his family, and his racketeering and mafia clan."

The Spark also surveys the situations in Egypt, Algeria, Yemen, Morocco, and Libya at the very beginning of the Arab Spring. Ben Jelloun writes, "The Arab Spring exploded victoriously mainly because the conditions were ripe. People spontaneously poured into the streets and decided to go all the way without following the orders of any political leader, party chief, or, much less, leaders of religious movements." Especially important in this book is Ben Jelloun's distinction between the words *revolt* and *revolution*. For him, a revolt occurs when people rise as one against a regime. Revolts often lack both formal organizations and recognized leaders. The Tunisian revolt is a good example as it began spontaneously when Bouazizi's desperate act was mis- or overinterpreted as the cue to demand the end to Ben Ali's dictatorial regime.

Ben Jelloun sees the Arab Spring as a string of revolts and not revolutions. In *The Spark* he makes a rough comparison between, for example, the Tunisian revolt and the Portuguese Carnation Revolution, which, in 1974, overthrew a forty-year-old dictatorship and gave people the right to vote, free health care, pensions for the elderly, and free public education. The Carnation Revolution was carefully planned and led by Otelo Saraiva de Carvalho. The junior officers of the military simply deposed their Portuguese superiors and set up a three-person junta that guided the country to democratic elections. The Carnation Revolution led to a new, democratic state with entitlements for virtually every class of people. The Portuguese were thrilled to have their repressive regime removed and to see instead respect for civil rights and the rule of law. The Arab Spring revolts, however, failed to have an outcome similar to the Carnation Revolution. Tunisia is the only nation in the region to have emerged from the Arab Spring with a democratic state. "Tunisians have shattered the dogma that citizens of the Arab world must either accept a secular authoritarian status quo or must submit to Islamist authoritarian rule" (Ryan 2014). The *New York Times* applauded Tunisia's achievement: "After a long and often fraught process, Tunisia has managed to produce the most liberal constitution in the Arab world, and it has done so through consensus" ("Tunisia's Remarkable Achievement" 2014). Then, in October 2015, a group of labor, business, legal- and human-rights activists called the National Dialogue Coalition won the Nobel Peace Prize. The Nobel committee cited the coalition's "decisive contribution to the building of a pluralistic democracy in Tunisia in the wake of the Jasmine Revolution of 2011" (Chan 2015).

There were earlier, occasional revolts in the Middle East and North Africa (MENA) region, but they were strongly repressed, and all the opponents were eliminated. Everything had been done to suppress the emergence of the individual as a singular entity. The French Revolution allowed French citizens to become individuals with rights and duties. "In the Arab world, it is the clan, the tribe, the family that is recognized, not the person as an individual," writes Ben Jelloun in *The Spark*. Yet, the individual is a voice, a person who has a say and who expresses his opinion by participating in free and fair elections. "That's what democracy is about: it's a culture based on a social contract," Ben Jelloun adds. "This is why," he contends about the Arab Spring, "it's not an ideological revolution." There was no leader, no guide, and no party to propel the revolution forward. It was millions of ordinary people who poured onto the street because they ran out of patience and tolerance. It is a new kind of revolution: spontaneous and improvised.

The Spark condemns Arab presidents who behave like absolute monarchs and stay in power by force, by corruption, and through lies and blackmail. Ben Jelloun argues that once leaders come to power, they think it is for eternity, whether the people want them or not. In order to appease the West, they establish a sort of "formal democracy." Everything's in their hands, though, and they will not tolerate any opposition. While in power, they do business, get rich, and keep their money in American or European banks. For Ben Jelloun, a crucial outcome of the Arab Spring is that dignity and honor have been restored to a whole generation. Arab citizens will no longer remain silent, submissive, and at the disposition of contemptuous power. Ben Jelloun hopes "an Arab man will become an individual who has a name, a voice, and all his rights" after the experience of the Arab Spring.

Wrapping up *The Spark*, Ben Jelloun tries to summarize the Arab Spring's aspirations, even if its reality fell short of the ideal. He writes,

What took place in Tunisia and Egypt is by nature moral and at the same time ethical. It's a full rejection, without compromise, of authoritarianism, corruption, theft of the country's resources, nepotism, favoritism, humiliation and illegitimacy that lie at the base of these leaders' coming to power and whose behavior is similar to the ways of the mafia. These protests bring a little bit of moral hygiene in a society that has been so exploited and humiliated. (*L'étincelle* 2011, 31–35)

When asked if he felt personally touched by the events, Ben Jelloun responded:

I am still affected by the events that are unfolding in the Arab world. I am appalled; I am angry; I am horrified by the massacres in Syria and by the impotence of the United Nations and the West. The Arab world is in the middle of a revolution; at the moment, we see only drama and blood. Perhaps something good will come out of all this—a real democracy, secularity, and a prosperity that will help the most destitute. (Treisman 2013)

Ben Jelloun cares deeply about politics, is interested in the Arab Spring and its future. Yet, he considers himself a writer only, not a political engagé: "I'm not a political writer. I am a citizen, concerned about politics, but I'm first and foremost a storyteller, a novelist, and a fabulator who plays with words and with the imaginary" (Triesman 2013).

Tahar Ben Jelloun: The Storyteller

Tahar Ben Jelloun is perhaps the contemporary Moroccan author best known in the United States, and he is one of the most translated, read, and studied Maghrebi writers in Europe. Shortlisted twice for the Nobel Prize in literature, Ben Jelloun is the recipient of many international literary awards including the Le Prix Goncourt in 1987 and the International IMPAC Dublin Literary Award in 2005. In his more than thirty-five works—which include novels, poetry collections, short-story collections, plays, many works of nonfiction, essays, meditations on current events, and documentary writings—he confronts and denounces corruption, exploitation, racial and gender discrimination, violence, and dictatorship. His interests stem from his youth in Morocco, where in 1966 he was sent to a military camp as a result of his participation in a rebellion against the repressive and violent acts of the

Moroccan police. It is at the camp that he started writing. His work is also informed by his education in psychology and experience as a psychotherapist.

Ben Jelloun was born to a family of modest means. Perhaps because he participated in the rebellion against the violent acts of the Moroccan police and was sent to a military camp as his punishment, he is in a position to understand the suffering of North Africans living difficult lives in what continues to be a difficult political environment with a high unemployment rate. Ben Jelloun is in a position to understand what Mohamed Bouazizi may have suffered under dictatorship.

Ben Jelloun's Ethics and Aesthetics

Translating an author of Tahar Ben Jelloun's stature demands that I know his ethical and aesthetic priorities, which, in turn, calls for thinking beyond the strictly biographical. French writer Jean-Marie Gustave Le Clézio said: "Tahar Ben Jelloun is a man the most concerned about time that I know. That is to say, time which passes, time which urges us on and engages us, and this time which is ours, sometimes so difficult and unjust" (Le Clézio 2000, 3). Ben Jelloun penetrates the superficial veneers of social practice to expose violence and injustice; he has firmly established himself as a writer who speaks for the socially marginal. Le Clézio calls Ben Jelloun, "the bearer of a very ancient wisdom, inherent from Moroccan civilization" (Le Clézio 2000, 4). He admires Ben Jelloun's natural elegance, his taste for sharing, and the seriousness with which he addresses himself to his audience. I too see Tahar Ben Jelloun as a humanist who often writes about the socially marginal and lends his voice to those who cannot speak, mostly to people of modest means.

During the Arab Spring revolts in 2011, Ben Jelloun went to the International Literature Festival in Berlin to talk about writers' ethical and aesthetic responsibilities. Katherine Sanders translated Ben Jelloun's remarks from the French in her brief essay, "Translating the Invisible with Tahar Ben Jelloun." The festival's keynote speaker, Ben Jelloun said, "We write out of the darkness that surrounds us." He believes that "to write about the world is to attempt to understand it better." He thinks it is important to listen to one's own people. For him, listening means being . . .

> willing to report the words and translate the silence of all those who hope and wait for someone to appear out of obscurity and tell the world of their suffering and to portray their future. . . . We need

the novel not only to explain the world to us, but also to accompany our historical times ... we must write more than ever ... beautifully, powerfully, even if humankind increasingly wallows in a pseudo-reality, in mediocrity, and in ugliness. (quoted in Sanders 2011)

In a world full of injustices, writers have a responsibility to be honest, yet doubt and imagination are also a part of literary works. "Ben Jelloun emphasized his opinion that both doubt and imagination need to be part of literature because they are part of life" (Sanders 2011). Ben Jelloun has doubts about Bouazizi's self-immolation being the main and only provocation of revolts in Tunisia. He has doubts that Bouazizi killed himself only because of police violence. *By Fire* flows from Ben Jelloun's moral imagination as an instrument of inquiry about the various levels and sources of pressure the historical Mohamed Bouazizi suffered.

Reading and Teaching *By Fire*

I read passages from *By Fire* at the American Literary Translator's Association's 2014 annual conference. As

I read, my voice caught. Looking up at the audience, I saw tears in their eyes. I realized at that precise moment the power words can have over us. I also realized the importance of literary translation. There are urgent stories out there that need to be told in as many languages as possible and made available to world readers. I also read the translation at SUNY Stony Brook's reading series. The university's Poetry Center was packed with professors and students. I was moved by the pin-drop silence while the audience learned about Mohamed's experience. For a moment, Mohamed was among us, and the audience could hear his voice. Many questions followed the reading. Perhaps because *By Fire* is based on a true story, it generates wide interest and has such a strong impact.

Reading the novella has had a strong effect on my students. They began writing research papers on the Arab Spring in January 2011 and have continued ever since. Their research turns up astonishing information about dictatorship, government corruption, police violence, and human rights abuses in the MENA region and elsewhere. Before reading *By Fire*, their essays were objective and journalistic reports. After spending time with the story, though, students write about corruption and human rights abuse with greater urgency, compassion, awareness, and concern. Bouazizi becomes more than a sterile historical figure; he is a devoted son, a caring brother, and a gentle lover, a man whom my students can understand and relate to.

Even so, I am intrigued that many of my students find fault with Mohamed's behavior and choices. "If it was the only way to make a living and take care of his family," they ask, "why didn't he bribe the police?" After all, they point out, Bouazizi bribed a travel agent to get an air-ticket refund. By killing himself, Mohamed deprived his family of essential support, which these students see as stubborn, selfish, reckless, and weak. They don't see him as a hero, but as a poor, desperate man whose self-immolation unwittingly triggered a revolt.

Some students do research on Ben Jelloun to understand more about why he wrote Bouazizi's story in the first place. They often wonder whether his motivation lay in his two-year military camp detention. Perhaps it is there, they often suggest, that he learned what it is to suffer at the hands of corrupt police.

What matters most to me is that *By Fire* provokes my students to ask questions. They want to know more about the writer, the historical Mohamed Bouazizi, the region, and the Arab Spring. The work has sparked student interest not only in the historical figure, but also the historical and political reasons behind the unprecedented Arab Spring movement. They want to know what became of the movement and how it relates to contemporary conflicts in the Middle East, North Africa, and beyond. Students' enthusiasm for engaging with Mohamed Bouazizi is the reason that my main objective in the classroom is generating their interest in global issues through global literature in English translation.

A Note on the Translation

After leaving the Paris bookstore with a copy of *By Fire*, I found a bench in Park Monceau and read the book without looking up. It was as though I did not even take a breath while I read. The sky had clouded over; it was already late afternoon. I closed the book and sat quietly for a while with my eyes closed, imagining those last few hours of Mohamed's life. I heard his desperate voice and felt an unusual urgency for Anglophone readers to encounter Mohamed as soon as possible. Without moving from my bench, I took out paper and pen and began translating. As I worked, images from Mohamed's life and death vividly unfolded before my eyes. Some of the passages left me trembling, breathless.

When I came across the following passage, Mohamed's

entire life, and then death, passed through my mind like sharp, clear snapshots:

A confused jumble of images rushed through his mind: His mother in bed, his father in his coffin, himself at the Faculty of Arts and Letters, Zineb smiling, Zineb angry, Zineb begging him not to do anything; his mother getting out of bed and calling for him; the face of the woman who had slapped him earlier, who slapped him again; his body bent forward as though he were offering himself to an executioner . . . his French teacher praising him; himself taking his college exams, showing his diploma to his parents; the diploma pinned to a sign beside the word *unemployed*; his diploma burning in the sink at his place; his father's burial again; screams; birds; the President and his wife wearing huge black sunglasses; the woman who had slapped him; the other who had insulted him . . . the police brutalizing him again; insults, blows, insults, blows . . .

I tried to imagine how he might have felt a moment before self-ignition. I decided to concentrate on Mohamed's agonized voice that spoke to me; I wanted to translate his stream of thoughts during those last days of his life.

Beyond *By Fire* and *The Spark*, I have translated and published several other works by Tahar Ben Jelloun, including his autobiographical novel *L'Ecrivain public* (*The Public Scribe*) and several short stories. What appealed to me when I first read Ben Jelloun is his language. His poetic French, which is so characteristic of most of his work, however, is a dramatic contrast with the writer's simple, direct, and straightforward language in *By Fire*. The plot moves fast, and so did my translation. Here, Ben Jelloun dispenses with superfluous details. Instead, he goes straight to the point. Nothing is left ambiguous, neither Mohamed's life nor his death. The writer himself said in his interview with the *New Yorker*, "Obviously the style had to be simple, direct, dry. The subject didn't allow for adjectives and flowers! I had to stick closely to the human being and to what he was going to do; I had to stay as close as I could to life and to death" (Treisman 2013).

Translating Mohamed's life and death was a deeply emotional experience. Recreating the text in English was stimulating; from French it flowed effortlessly into English. Troublesome were certain French idiomatic expressions and slang words. A few other words and phrases were difficult to translate either because they are cognates with different meanings in French and English or because the concepts do not exist in English. The word *concierge*, used for the receptionist at the town hall, for example, has a different meaning in French than it does in English. I translated it as "man at the front desk," or "the front-desk clerk." I translated phrases like *camarade de lute* as "fellow activist," *un député de la majorité* as "MP," and *des diplômés chômeurs* as "unemployed graduates"—words and a concept not as widespread in the West as in the MENA region.

Another word is *rial*, which Ben Jelloun uses as the local currency in *Par le feu*. I found this odd when I first read the book. *Rial* is Iranian, Omani, and Yemeni currency, not Tunisian. Later, Ben Jelloun confirmed to me his intention of portraying his Mohamed as any Mohamed from any Arab country. Ben Jelloun uppercases *P* for *President* (which I have left in uppercase), even when not preceding a proper noun like Ben Ali. I believe his use of the uppercase *P* is to show the fear and reverence the characters feel, especially government officials, when they speak about their president. Overall, there are few untranslatable lexical choices or constructions in *Par le feu*, and even fewer in *L'étincelle*. In *The Spark*, Ben Ali says at one point, "Yes, I, the Raïs—I have cried." The word *Raïs* is a title used by the rulers of Arab states in the Middle East. Though it is translated as "president," I have kept the original word.

I have strived to preserve Ben Jelloun's tone and diction, his compassion for the protagonist, and his representation of Mohamed's toxic environment. Priorities in my translation were faithfulness to the text's lexical choices, Ben Jelloun's aesthetic, and his voice, which is unique among Arab writers. I have sought to preserve the essence of idiomatic expressions. Above all, by respecting its cultural sensibilities, I have resisted domesticating the text, as an American Englishing will not tolerate Ben Jelloun's voice. In *Par le feu*, there appears several times the word *flic*, whose translation is "cop"; I chose "police" or "police officer," and used the word *cop* only in dialogue. I left all cultural elements and sensibilities intact as readers depend on them for access to Ben Jelloun's streets full of vendors fleeing security agents, parrot men, sellers of pirated DVDs and loose American cigarettes, acrobats performing tricks, monkey trainers, storytellers, drivers who stop to buy fruit through the car window, and town halls where front-desk clerks repel people like Mohamed.

Translators have an especially important task when they undertake texts from acutely inflamed areas of the world. Literary texts and their translations *can* open for readers the work of writers who bring news from a space unseen and unseeable by television cameras and officials' sound bites. The Arab Spring is perhaps history, yet conditions throughout the Middle East continuously plunge into overwhelming humanitarian crises. Human rights abuses run rampant as beheadings and legions of starving, exploited refugees dominate news from the region. The chaos of war and the continuously shifting allegiances of sects, clans, and rebels birth rumors and confusion. There are stories of illegal emigrants making treacherous journeys to find employment, and there are stories of many young Tunisians and European Muslims joining the so-called Islamic State.

Then there are the Mohamed Bouazizis embedded in this mélange of violence and irrationality. They do not want to fight. They want to feed their families and live in peace and dignity. Ben Jelloun tells the story of one such man whom his government failed. Then the sky fell in. Hopes soared for a new era with the Arab Spring, and they collapsed. Now, more than ever, continuous war appears to be the new normal. Beneath the smoke and the rubble, the collapsed homes and desperate refugees, there are real people—individuals, not groups. Redeeming the individual sufferer amid the masses that the West sees on its iPhones and iPads is Ben Jelloun's moral imperative. Neither the historical Mohamed Bouazizi nor his double are Everyman. Rather than generalize, though, Ben Jelloun, through the double he creates *as an act of literature*, reveals Mohamed Bouazizi in all his specificity.

Translation is an art. It requires creativity. Above all, it offers understanding of the global perspective. Translating *By Fire* and *The Spark* was not a process of replacing one word with another. It meant capturing the essence of the texts. The translation process and recreation of the texts fostered in me a sense of empathy like I never experienced before. It offered me a deeper understanding of how people like Mohamed might feel. I translate Tahar Ben Jelloun's stories because they help me understand the human condition. I translate his work because he confronts and denounces dictatorship, corruption, exploitation, violence, and female repression. Like the author himself who speaks for all those who cannot speak, I want to translate the silence of all those who hope and wait for someone to tell the world of their suffering. Ben Jelloun's achievement is to peel back the West's layers of culture, fear, suspicion, distance, and apathy, and allow us to see—to really see, in a way that only art enables—one specific son, brother, and lover in his humiliation, desperation, and death.

Bibliography

Beaumont, Peter. 2011. "Mohammed Bouazizi: The Dutiful Son Whose Death Changed Tunisia's Fate." *Guardian* (London), January 20. Accessed November 19, 2014.

Ben Jelloun, Tahar. 2011. *L'étincelle*. Paris: Gallimard.

———. 2011. *Par le feu: Récit*. Paris: Gallimard.

———. 2013. "By Fire." Translated by Rita S. Nezami. *New Yorker*, September 16.

Chan, Sewell. 2015. "Nobel Peace Prize Is Awarded to National Dialogue Quartet in Tunisia." *New York Times*, October 9. Accessed December 9, 2015.

DeLillo, Don. 1993. "The Art of Fiction." Interview by Adam Begley. *Paris Review*, Summer. Accessed November 2, 2014.

Kundera, Milan, and Michael Henry Heim. 1981. *The Book of Laughter and Forgetting*. Translated by Michael Heim. New York: Penguin.

Le Clézio, J. M. G. 2000. "Tahar the Wise." *Banipal: Magazine of Modern Arab Literature* 8 (Summer): 3–5.

"Memories of a Tunisian Martyr." 2011. BBC News, January 22. Accessed October 27, 2014.

"Q&A: Tunisia Crisis." 2011. *BBC News*, January 19. Accessed November 30, 2014.

"Religious Views on Suicide." N.d. *Muslim Public Affairs Council*. MPAC Foundation. Accessed November 18, 2014.

Ryan, Yasmine. 2014. "How One Country Emerged from the Arab Spring with a Democratic State." *Nation*, March 3. Accessed November 16, 2014.

Sanders, Katherine. 2011. "Translating the Invisible with Tahar Ben Jelloun." *Words without Borders*, September 27. Accessed October 30, 2014.

Simon, Bob. 2011. "How a Slap Sparked Tunisia's Revolution." *CBS Interactive*, February 22. Accessed October 27, 2014.

Thomas, Anne. 2011. "Authors at Berlin Festival Talk about 'Writing the Arab Spring.'" *Deutsche Welle*, September 13. Accessed November 26, 2014.

Treisman, Deborah. 2013. "This Week in Fiction: Tahar Ben Jelloun." *New Yorker*, September 6. Accessed October 30, 2014.

"Tunisia Country Profile." 2007. *Carter Center*, August. Accessed December 8, 2015.

"Tunisia: Neighbor's Duty." 1957. *Time*, December 2, 1–2. Accessed November 27, 2014.

"Tunisia: No Time for Democracy." 1958. *Time*, September 29, 2. Accessed November 27, 2014.

"Tunisia Revolt: Mohamed Bouazizi Police Suspect Freed." 2011. *BBC News*, April 20.

"Tunisia's Remarkable Achievement." 2014. *New York Times*, January 28. Accessed December 8, 2015.

Waltz, Susan Eileen. 1995. *Human Rights and Reform: Changing the Face of North African Politics*. Berkeley: University of California Press.

BY FIRE

THE SPARK

TUNISIA

December 2010–January 2011

The Tunisian national anthem by poet Aboul Qacem Echebbi ends with these four lines:

When the people will to live,
Destiny must surely respond.
Oppression shall then vanish.
Fetters are certain to break.

The demonstrators sang this verse, as had their grandparents, during the fight for independence in 1956.

Ben Ali's regime could be compared to a colonial occupation; that is to say, illegitimate and cruel. He spent more than twenty years assembling networks and structures that rendered the country at his mercy. Using the pretext of protecting the country from the Islamist peril, he allowed himself anything that pleased him, all under the watchful and encouraging eyes of European nations.

Revolutions and resistance often inspire a surge of creativity in poets. After Tunisia embraced new ways of living and working, Egypt followed with a revolt that subverted the idea that the Arab region is cursed and doomed to dictatorship and regression. Some writers devoted their lives to denouncing this curse. Always visionaries, poets foresee what absolutely must change. Dictators would do well to read the poets, whom, in general, they hate. A day always arrives when people's resistance itself becomes a kind of poem. We saw it in the streets of Tunisia and then in Egypt.

Today, we're still talking about the collapse of Berlin's immense wall. Other walls, other taboos, and other oppressions continue crumbling at this moment. Poets were among the first to see what might happen: the Russian Vladimir Mayakovski, the Turk Nazim Hikmet, the Palestinian Mahmoud Darwish, the Iraqi Shakir al-Sayyab, the Egyptian Ahmed Chawki—each in his own way raised his voice during the last century to reveal the intolerable and the vital need for freedom and justice. Yet, no authoritarian regime took seriously what a poet or an artist had to say about society.

Everybody knew what the police were doing in Arab countries; the international media often spoke about the repression whose victims were the common people, the destitute, the forgotten, and all those who suffered from injustice but couldn't speak for or defend themselves. Many journalists or exiled militants wrote books that denounced dictators, yet these dictators were "acceptable" for Western leaders, who were too tolerant. But isolated voices can never bring down dictators; it took many incidents, clashes with the police, glaring injustices, and intolerable acts for the spark to finally ignite.

This is how people live in developing countries. This is how they die in countries where, in the eyes of the West, stability and security are guaranteed, although the people are denied their freedom and rights.

Everyone supported Ben Ali's takeover in the late 1980s. They even called it a "medical coup d'état." On a beautiful morning on November 7, 1987, the person whom Habib Bourguiba had named minister of interior, and then prime minister, entered the palace and forced the sick old man out of his bed and informed him that he was no longer the president. The day before, Ben Ali had assembled seven doctors at the Ministry of Interior and obliged them to sign a certificate attesting to "Bourguiba's incapacity to govern." It is said that one of the doctors who didn't want to sign, as he hadn't seen Bourguiba for ten years, was ordered by Ben Ali: "Sign. You don't have a choice." For some time, Ben Ali had placed his own henchmen in the ministries. He got rid of a great man and shamelessly took his place. Bourguiba, of course, could have decided to leave power on his own if his health condition didn't allow him to govern anymore. But once one has tasted power, one acts as though infected by a virus. Only Léopold Sédar Senghor, president of Senegal, left office voluntarily, to dedicate his time to writing, poetry, and reading. To say the least, not all heads of nations are poets—far from it!

LET'S NOW REMEMBER Bourguiba's audacity and sense of modernity. Above all, he negotiated with France for his country's independence. Straightaway, he led Tunisia on a path to modernity that was rare in the Arab world at that time. He changed the personal status code—Tunisia was the first, and, for a long time, the only Muslim and Arab nation to recognize women's rights: polygamy was forbidden, divorce was authorized, and abortion legalized (long before France!). It was revolutionary. Bourguiba was the only leader to publicly advocate secularism: on a day during Ramadan in March 1964, he gave a live television presentation during which he drank a glass of orange juice in front of amazed viewers. He justified his gesture by invoking economic reasons. He said he couldn't tolerate the country's economy going to sleep for an entire month, because by fasting, workers have neither the strength nor the energy to do their work well. During the decades in which Bourguiba ruled, Tunisians were free to fast or not to fast. Cafés and restaurants remained open. People could eat in peace. No one reproached or bothered those who fasted due to religious convictions.

Bourguiba gave a visionary speech on March 3, 1965, in Jericho, but no one could accept it at that time. He advised Arabs to "normalize their relationship with the state of Israel," claiming "the politics of everything or nothing brought the Palestinians nothing but defeat." He antagonized all the Arab heads of state, especially Egypt's Gamal Abdel Nasser, whom he criticized for his fanatical nationalism. The people in Arab countries protested in the streets against the capitulation of a "traitor to the sacred cause of Palestine." This didn't dissuade Bourguiba from demanding that the United Nations "create a federation among the Arab states in the region and Israel."

Two years later, on June 5, 1967, Israel launched a sudden war against Egypt, Syria, Jordan, and Iraq. *Naqba*, meaning catastrophe, is the Arabic name they gave to their defeat. Today, the Palestinians might dream of getting back their territory from before June 1967 . . . but Israel will never give them even a square meter.

Bourguiba was secular, educated, and a visionary man. His authoritative temperament damaged his image. He was, despite his reforms, an unjust president, particularly to those who democratically opposed his politics. But was it a sufficient reason for Ben Ali, a military man married to a hairdresser, to dispose of him like a decaying body awaiting death?

BEN ALI DIDN'T MAKE radical changes when he first took power. He continued Bourguiba's reforms, particularly in the field of education. He consulted Mohamed Charfi, a human rights activist, and put him in charge of the Ministry of National Education with the aim to cleanse textbooks of Islamist and fanatical ideology. With a team of about fifty professors, Mohamed Charfi did remarkable work. He rewrote all the textbooks in the spirit of the Enlightenment and open-mindedness. Ben Ali encouraged his work. As soon as the work was completed, though, Mohamed Charfi resigned and disassociated himself from the Ben Ali government.

The fight against Islamic fundamentalists rapidly became one of Ben Ali's obsessions; it turned into a witch hunt, involving arbitrary arrests and torture at police stations in the worst possible conditions imaginable. Under the pretext of the Islamist threat, Ben Ali became more and more dictatorial, instilling fear in the country, forbidding the foreign press, hunting down opponents, even those who had nothing to do with Islamism. The country's economic growth and its appearance to the West as a fortress of stability—even at the cost of repression—rapidly framed Ben Ali as a reassuring "rampart against Islamism." That's how, during three decades, Ben Ali was able to subject his country, without any opposition, to a dictatorship that strictly denied Tunisians any rights. Tunisia became his private affair. His family, in the strict and broad senses, profited from the country excessively and shamelessly. Paris officials released one of Ben Ali's brothers, caught red-handed trafficking drugs in France; he calmly returned to his golden villa in Tunis. At the same moment, activists were getting arrested. Graduates, young and jobless, roamed the streets rather than swell the ranks of illegal immigrants.

Tunisia and its president, who got himself reelected every five years with up to 90 percent of the vote, always enjoyed good ratings from Western embassies. During his official visits to Europe, Ben Ali was applauded and celebrated, and his country was recognized as an optimistic example of "making progress toward democracy." It was beyond belief. When he fled as a thief from Tunisia (because he was a thief), TV channels rebroadcast talks by Jacques Chirac, Nicolas Sarkozy, Dominique Strauss-Kahn, Silvio Berlusconi, and others. It was frightening to hear what these people said in front of Ben Ali, and baffling when they were at a loss for words when the thug ran away. This is called "realpolitik."

Thanks to Tunisia's positive image, the country gradually became a popular tourist destination. This helped boost the country's economy and employment. Tourists couldn't see any of the regime's scandalous aspects; it took an informed journalist or an attentive writer to see these traits. I first experienced them in 2005. I was invited to give a talk to university and high school students at the invitation of the French Cultural Center of Tunisia. Before long, I noticed that civilian-clothed police officers were continuously following me. The students asked strictly literary questions, but as soon as the talk was over, they came to see me and spoke in whispers. I hated this trip and the leaden atmosphere. Journalists who dared denounce this hyper–police state were simply imprisoned. The best known among them, Taoufik Ben Brik, spent six months in prison during 2009 and 2010 after a trial built totally on lies. The regime found intolerable his outspokenness and criticism against the regime, especially regarding torture and disappearance of opponents.

The bombing of the synagogue in Djerba on April 11, 2002, that left twenty-one dead made the most vigilant observers realize that even though Ben Ali managed to keep the Islamists at bay in his country, his police didn't succeed in stopping al-Qaida from committing bloody acts on his land. The suicide bomber came from an immigrant family in France and had connections with a German who had converted to Islam . . .

The Spark

I had never heard about the small town of Sidi Bouzid. Yet, it's there that it all started. Even though the incident was common and banal, this time it ended by triggering the irrevocable.

There was once a young man of twenty-eight, who had degrees but no job. He lived with his mother, brothers, and sisters. To make a little money, he got himself a fruit stand, a kind of cart on which vendors put seasonal fruit and vegetables to sell. Street vendors. We see them everywhere in Maghrebi cities. Often, cars stop or double park in front of them to buy last-minute fruit as dessert for lunch. These vendors can't afford to have a store. They are poor and live from day to day. Sometimes their carts get in the way of the traffic, but everyone makes do. And, if a vendor "buys" the neighborhood police officer's favor, he is left in peace and can sell his produce without being harassed. At times though, the same police officer, eager to demonstrate his strictness to his supervisor, is excessively zealous and forces the vendor to sell his produce elsewhere. Some spots are better located than others—those with more traffic are obviously better for selling. For these spots, one has to "pay." Slipping one or two banknotes to a police officer is indispensable. The relationship between the police and vendors is one of the dominating and dominated, not unlike the small neighborhood mafias in Italy. You want to work? Well, you have to pay. If the vendor refuses, his cart is knocked over or confiscated for causing "trouble in the public thoroughfare."

The amount of money a street vendor makes is not huge. It's hardly enough to feed a small family. No one has ever seen a fruit and vegetable street vendor make a fortune. Mohamed Bouazizi was one of these people who toil every day to try to live in dignity. He refused to beg or accept the mafia compromises, to steal or do anything that is illegal. He could see very well how Ben Ali and his large family, his own and his wife's, took advantage of the country shamelessly. Like all Tunisians, Mohamed knew about the lawlessness of Ben Ali's in-laws, brothers, brothers-in-law, cousins, and friends, and how this pack's members didn't bother hiding while they made millions. All the big businesses, all big companies, and all foreign investments had to go through the "Ben Ali–Trabelsi law." Everyone knew about this system; they talked about it, and then said, "We'll close our eyes to it because Tunisia is finished with Islamists." The well-off, middle-class people of Tunis, La Marsa, Sidi Bou-Saïd, and Hammamet boasted of living in a country "with perfect security," "without robberies or attacks in the streets, where the police do their job really well." People who collaborated with the regime enjoyed remarkable comfort and well-being. They were grateful to Ben Ali, this former military man, who knew so well how to capitalize on his country's wealth. French and Italian politicians often viewed Tunisia as exemplary in the Arab-Muslim world. The Islamist leader Rached Ghannouchi took refuge in London. No one heard about him or his Ennahda movement anymore. Islamism was buried.

Mohamed Bouazizi had to stop his studies because his father died. Mohamed's father was a farmworker. Mohamed has to take care of his entire family of seven. He buys a cart to sell fruit and vegetables in the street. However, he doesn't have authorization from the police. The police harass him, but he refuses to give in to corruption. In any case, he doesn't have the means. The police don't leave him alone. As soon as they see him, they go after him, threatening to confiscate his cart and weighing scale. On this morning of December 17, 2010, he comes across a group of particularly mean police officers who confiscate his cart. One of the officers is a woman; she slaps him, and another spits on him. Supreme humiliation. He tries to get his cart back, explaining that he has seven people to feed and that he hasn't done anything wrong. . . . The police officers' aggressiveness doubles in ferocity. Mohamed's anger rises, and he decides to talk to someone in the town hall; no one wants to listen to him. He then goes to the governorate. . . . At that moment, no one knew that this humiliation would lead to the spark of a revolt with immeasurable consequences . . .

SOME SPEND THEIR LIVES swallowing affronts, rationalizing and accepting their fates; they keep telling themselves that light will return one day even though life is nothing but an accumulation of disasters. They hope, they pray, they look elsewhere: the beauty of trees, the flight of a bird, the flutter of a butterfly, the smile on a child's face, and they feel a sudden burst of confidence in humanity; they tell themselves things will get better, that it's just a bad moment, that God is merciful and will open doors. But on that day, Mohamed felt he was banging his head against a concrete wall. He saw no way out of his fate. He couldn't see any compassion in the eyes of passersby. Not a single hand reached out, not a word of encouragement, no justice. Mohamed is a citizen of the world who has reached the end of his patience. Yet, he could have thought about the character of Ayoub—about Job in the Koran—and the patience he had to demonstrate to endure all God had inflicted on him. But Mohamed didn't think about him. Job is far away. Everyone is far away. There's no one around him. He can't even feel the presence of his mother or his sister, Leïla, whom he loves very much. He feels isolated, abandoned. God has abandoned him. Now he's sure about that. On this cold December morning, he looks at the sky. Nobody gives him the slightest sign. Absolute solitude deepened by a cruel sense of unbearable injustice. The slap and then the spitting. One doesn't do this, not even to a dog. He's been stripped of his humanity much as a woman wipes makeup from her face. His face is no longer visible, his eyes can no longer see, and his self-esteem is gone. His dignity has been crushed beneath police boots. He tells himself, "It's crazy how the poor are mean to each other, to those who are even poorer." Because these police officers are miserable, they turn to corruption; they become servile and behave like slaves when the governor calls them to bring a cup of coffee or when they are told to paint his villa. They obey; they bend over to serve the authority. They lower their heads and eyes to serve those who have given them a job. Everyone knows that. Being indebted is a modern form of slavery. So, they do more than their duty. They take initiatives and see themselves as small chiefs, but chiefs anyway. They give orders with the same arrogance, the same violence that their supervisors use on them. A poor street vendor becomes an ideal victim. They can despise him because they have power over him; they can confiscate his cart, and if he's not happy, let him die. "Ah! Let him croak!" These, apparently, were the words spoken by Ben Ali when he found out the street vendor had self-immolated.

Mohamed Bouazizi endured fifteen days and fifteen nights of suffering before dying. Like a dog, like a "nobody at all," like a nameless shadow, like a poor man. Being poor in Tunisia, Egypt, Yemen, and various other countries means being destined to croak like a dog, either because a police officer will push you to commit suicide or when you get sick, you won't be treated and you'll die from lack of medicine and medical assistance.

Mohamed Bouazizi decided to end his life. But how could he bring himself to self-immolate by fire? This is certainly not part of the Maghrebi tradition and culture, nor part of Islam, which forbids it. The one who defies God by taking his own life will repeat the same act for infinity. Mohamed must have seen images of monks self-immolating; or perhaps he heard about it. This act is spectacular; it's directly significant and without ambiguity. Fire leaves nothing. It destroys everything. It inflicts terrible agony. Mohamed set himself on fire in public, in front of the town hall, in front of this government building that refused to listen to him and do him justice. He knew he had lost his cart for good, that the police would never return it, that their superiors wouldn't take his side and help him. He knew that the poor in his country are condemned just for being poor. So his despair must lead to something that could, perhaps, capture the attention of the indifferent, those who were unjust, those who were powerless to do anything other than protect their own interests, and those who were oblivious to the fate of a street vendor.

Hang himself at home? That would serve nothing . . . Cut his veins? Not that either . . . Fill himself with sleeping pills? He can't afford to buy them, and also, that would be a silent suicide; people would say: the poor man, he had a peaceful death . . . death in his sleep! No, Mohamed wanted to die and make his death become a useful act for others, useful for the poor, useful for the country. Perhaps he didn't think at all about his country, but while dousing himself with gasoline and clicking a lighter, he must have had the time to think about his mother, his brothers and sisters, maybe also about his father; he must have thought it's better to join his father instead of living in humiliation, without dignity, without money, victim of small bastards' whims; their venom is as terrible as that of big bastards.

The fire ignited instantly. He didn't move. When people ran to save him, it was too late. The fire was faster than they were; the fire had done its job. Mohamed was still breathing, but it was the breath of a charred body, a body whose soul already smelled the perfume of heaven, or, perhaps, the flames of hell. He was transported to a hospital in Sfax, then to the Burn Center in Ben Arous near Tunis. The body started to crackle. The soul couldn't get out, trapped by ash and held prisoner in a body that was no longer a body, but an example of what humiliation can provoke.

His body lay on the hospital bed wrapped in bandages. Many hoped that, magically, the bandages would suddenly unroll before their eyes and the TV cameras, and that, little by little, a frail, new body would appear in its place as though propelled by an angel or a god who would have mercy on this poor man, a man who had just sacrificed his life for about 11 million people.

On December 19, the people of Sidi Bouzid started demonstrating. This was the beginning of what later came to be known as the Jasmine Revolution.

A few days later, on December 28, Ben Ali visited Mohamed Bouazizi, who was glued to the hospital bed. These were grotesque images of a president trying to appear paternal, but having the air of someone inwardly cursing this poor bastard whose action triggered the first demonstrations. But this man, whose body has turned into that of a mummy, won't be here for long. He dies on January 4. Ten days later, Ben Ali's regime gives up the ghost. The president flees, begs for asylum here and there, and then ends up going to Jeddah, land of Islam that cannot refuse hospitality to a Muslim. As for his wife and family, they're already far away.

That's how Mohamed Bouazizi unwittingly became a hero. His sacrifice had been worthwhile. This was, no doubt, what he had hoped for, but neither he nor anyone else could have foreseen what followed. With calm and dignity, Tunisians rose as one. It was the police who were violent; their brutality left several dozen dead and hundreds of others wounded. Submissive for twenty-three years to a quiet dictatorship, the people succeeded in bringing down Ben Ali, his family, and his racketeering and mafia clan.

In 2009, BEN ALI had taken office again with a ridiculously low and humiliating number of votes. (He, though, claimed that more than 89 percent of the citizens elected him. The people felt mocked and held in contempt.) According to a reliable source, only 24.7 percent of Tunisian voters went to the polling locations. The petition, signed a few months later by important people in the eyes of the regime, encouraged Ben Ali to run again in 2014. It was really grotesque. We now know more precisely the extent of harm that Ben Ali caused. According to the February 7, 2011, edition of the Tunisian newspaper, *La Presse*, the regime hid from the people the real rate of unemployment, immigration, academic failure, and so on. According to the same newspaper, the unemployment rate among college graduates was 44.9 percent, while the rate among the youth of age eighteen to twenty-nine was 29.8 percent; more than 1 million high school students dropped out between 2004 and 2009. Finally, 70 percent of young Tunisians admitted wanting to emigrate by any means.

More important than the Ben Ali regime's abuses, which continue to be uncovered, is that Bouazizi's death helped establish Tunisia as an exemplar of political change in the Arab world. People were justified in describing this event as a conflagration with contagious effects. In the weeks following Mohamed Bouazizi's death, Egyptians took up Tunisia's example despite their more powerful and fierce Raïs.

Inside Ben Ali's Head

While Mubarak has a headache, what is Ben Ali, the Tunisian, who fled from his country on January 14, doing? He exiled himself in Saudi Arabia. European banks froze a part of his wealth, as well as all his real-estate holdings in France (his own and that of his clan); he must prove that they were acquired with clean money, such as his salary, for example. One of his private jets was also detained in France at the Bourget Airport.

What does he do with his days? He watches television. He just lies around. He doesn't feel like coloring his hair. He is depressed. He lives in a gilded prison. He is not able to go out even for a coffee in the nearest shopping center. He would like to cry. He sees again Mohamed Bouazizi's bandaged body and curses him. Ben Ali doesn't believe in God anymore. It's because God sides with the poor at present, with people in Mohamed Bouazizi's condition. "It took that idiot to get carried away by anger, set his clothes on fire, so that I, who brought prosperity to Tunisians, today find myself in this palace, alone, without friends, without my toys, without anything! Also, these television channels around the world will say anything. My head is filled with all sorts of images, but the journalists care only about *fawda*, the disorder and panic. Revolution? In reality, it's just chaos. They're going to destroy everything in this beautiful country. At least, I managed to bring millions of tourists; I created a middle class; I got rid of the Islamists; I worked to reassure the West, and now everybody's turning away from me. Human beings are ungrateful. I hate humanity. I hate this palace, this excessive air conditioning, and these Kleenex boxes with golden covers. I hate this yellow and white landscape, and I don't like the food. But I couldn't care less; I'm not hungry. This son of a bitch Bouazizi has destroyed my life. The country wanted chaos; well, they've got it. If this is what they like, let them enjoy it. These people are ungrateful and cowards. They bent over backward when they came to me for a job or favor. Today they swagger! Poor guys! They're pathetic! Doing this to me, who has sacrificed myself for them! They have been slow to wake up. Assholes, men without balls. If God exists, if the last Day of Judgment exists, there will be an extraordinary confrontation.

"People think a leader of a nation is made of iron, of stainless steel. I have a heart; I have feelings. I love gardens and rose bouquets. I love the sweetness of life and the sunset on La Marsa.

"I wept with emotion when my grandchildren were born. Yes, I, the Raïs—I have cried. Today, my tears have dried up. I feel rage and hatred inside me. I made a mistake. I was ill-advised. I should have fought like Gaddafi. He's crazy, but he doesn't shed tears; he doesn't abdicate.

"Gaddafi has ruled ten years longer than me. He has become richer than Mubarak and me together. He stands up to the entire world. His madness leads him to victory. Killing hundreds of Libyans means nothing to him; what matters to Gaddafi is saving his own skin and not ending up in front of a court, as did Saddam Hussein. I'll never forget Saddam's face on the day when he was found hiding in a hole. He looked like someone awakened in the middle of the night, running his hands through his hair as though looking for lice, checking the condition of his teeth . . . What humiliation!

"As for me, I could never imagine leaving my country and begging for asylum. At least, I escaped a humiliating capture in front of the CNN and Al Jazeera cameras. If we have fallen, it's because of the undermining propaganda of the Muslim Brotherhood, who took hold of Al Jazeera from the beginning. The emir of Qatar is clever, or, rather, it's his wife, Sheikha Mozah. She's the one who had the idea for this TV channel. She's the one who has killed us. Obviously, there was never a word on this channel about the situation in Qatar. On the other hand, every little incident in other Arab countries is exposed and televised over and over again. The whole plan came from this channel. By repeating that this or that person is a dictator, people ended up believing it. I must admit that my sons-in-law, sons of the nouveau riche, didn't help my situation. As for my wife, she went overboard and wanted to possess and control everything. No man in Tunisia is capable of saying *no* to his wife when she decides to take over. I'm speaking from experience. I kept telling her, 'Be careful. Tell your nephew not to overdo it; someday it'll end badly . . .' But no, like me she believed that this life in which everything is allowed is eternal. Everything was going well. The country was calm. The police headquarters and officers did their work discreetly. Foreign press couldn't enter the country. Tourists loved Djerba and Tozeur. But now, a gang of thugs, agitated by the unemployed, the rascals, and the loafers, has come to destroy all this. The elders used to say, 'The Arab must be crushed, or else he will crush you.' I hadn't been attentive enough to their wisdom."

THE NEW TUNISIAN CONSTITUTION IS REVOLUTIONARY

The tree of the Arab Spring has yielded its first fruits in Tunisia. This is the first time that an Arab and Muslim country has included in its new constitution equality between men and women ("male and female citizens are equal before the law without discrimination"). At the same time, the country has managed to put aside the Sharia law by establishing freedom of conscience ("the State is the guardian of religion. It guarantees freedom of conscience and freedom of worship"). The state also guarantees freedom of expression and prohibits physical and mental torture ("torture is an imprescriptible crime").

Not only has Tunisia—thanks to the commitment of its civil society, especially through the struggle of women—managed to drive the Islamist party Ennahda into mosques, but at the same time it has opened the country to a modernity that is sorely lacking in the rest of the Arab world. Equal rights means that there will be no polygamy or repudiation (the unilateral right of a husband to verbally divorce his wife); it also means that inheritance law will no longer follow the Islamic law that systematically gives the woman half of the man's share. Sura 4, verse 12 says: "As for your children, God commands you to assign [the male] a share equal to that of two females."

Steps toward equality are being made in the realm of employment and wages. In Europe, a man is still paid more than a woman for the same work. Maybe Tunisia will set an example by upsetting the norm and by getting rid of prejudices and archaism.

Equal rights between men and women are precisely what the Islamists cannot accept. It's because in politics what lies behind the use of religion is the fear of women, fear of the liberated woman's sexuality, fear that the man may lose the supremacy that some [Koranic] verses attribute to him. Religious fundamentalism is obsessed with sex. This is why a man seeks to veil a woman whether she is his wife, sister, or mother. He must hide her, make her invisible. He must suffocate her desire because all the problems of society arise, according to the fundamentalists, from women's liberation. Fundamentalists criticize the West where they believe liberalization of morals has caused the disintegration of the family.

The struggle for the liberation of the Tunisian man and woman doesn't date from yesterday. Admittedly, it was the former President Habib Bourguiba (1903–2000) who launched in the sixties the program for the liberation of Tunisian society. He was the first in the Arab world to implement a progressive family code. The Tunisian personal status code [equality between women and men], which dates from August 13, 1956, was an essential step toward modernity. Then came an attempted secularization of society. Bourguiba had the courage to appear on television one day during Ramadan and say, while drinking a glass of orange juice, that "Tunisia is fighting for its economic development. Ramadan gets in the way of this fight. During war, soldiers are allowed to eat and drink. Consider that we are at war for development." Those who refused to renounce their religious beliefs were free to practice their faith. The others were free to eat and drink publicly. It was a historic decision. Today, such a decision would cause violent demonstrations. Religion has become too important in people's lives because of frustration and political deception. This is why the new Tunisian Constitution marks an important date in the history of a spring that almost turned into a winter nightmare. But everything hasn't played out yet. It is also necessary that the legislative and presidential elections confirm this progress at the polls. The game is not over yet. The forces of regression are not disarmed. Salafis have not disappeared from the Tunisian landscape, and, occasionally, they reappear and attack the police or citizens who live freely. Their movement, "Ansar al Sharia" ("Defenders of

Sharia"), led by a veteran of the war in Afghanistan, the Tunisian Abu Iyade, was classified by the government as a "terrorist organization."

If Tunisia consolidates the changes in the constitution and manages to put them into practice, the entire Arab world will condemn the country—especially its neighbor Algeria, which has the most retrograde family code in the Maghreb. As for Morocco, although it amended its personal status code, it did not dare touch the Sharia inheritance law.

Gulf countries, including Saudi Arabia and Qatar, follow the Wahhabi belief, which is a rigid and retrograde dogma dating from the eighteenth century. Today, Saudi women fight for the right to drive a car; their country continues to apply the Sharia law. The hypocritical West likes to sign lucrative contracts with these countries and pretends not to know that it deals with champions of retrograde practices. We will see in the near future how these countries react to the historical turning point of Tunisia, an exceptional nation that has embraced the path of secularism. Tunisia's reforms do not reject religion, but separate the public and private spheres where people are free to believe or not to believe. The new Tunisian Constitution also prohibits charges of apostasy. In Egypt, for example, citizens who had an unorthodox reading of the Koran could be sentenced to death. These citizens were condemned as apostates whose crime was unpardonable from the Islamic point of view.

This was the case for the Egyptian historian Nasr Hamid Abu Zayd (1943–2000), whom the Egyptian court pursued for proposing a critical reading of Islamic texts. He was declared an apostate by the court, which annulled his marriage to a Muslim woman. (An apostate is considered someone who leaves the house of Islam; thus, a Muslim woman cannot be the wife of a non-Muslim.) Abu Zayd and his wife exiled themselves and settled in the Netherlands, where he died in 2000. He is often cited as an example of an intellectual who dared promote modern and critical thinking in Islam. Any critical interpretation of religion is severely punished, at least by the University of Al Azhar in Cairo.

Paris, 2015

BY FIRE

1.

Returning home from the cemetery where he just buried his father, Mohamed felt as though the burden he carried had become heavier. He was bent, aged, and walked slowly. He had just turned thirty. Never celebrated his birthday. The years went by and they were all alike. Poverty, deprivation, and a vague resignation imbued his life with a sadness that had, over time, come to seem natural. Like his father, he never complained. He was not a fatalist, or even religious.

His father's death turned his life upside down. He was the eldest, and was thus responsible now for the family. Three brothers and two sisters. A diabetic mother, but not yet an invalid. Mohamed's latest job hunt, like many before, had yielded nothing. Now he was nervous. It wasn't a question of being lucky or unlucky. It was more, he said, a problem of injustice, linked to the misfortune of being born poor. He was not going to sit in front of the

Finance Ministry's headquarters to protest unemployment any longer. Some formerly unemployed graduates had found work, but he wasn't one of them. His degree in history didn't interest anyone. He could have taught, but the Ministry of National Education wasn't hiring anymore.

He dug out his old schoolbag, hidden in the linen closet, emptied it of all its papers and documents, including his diploma, made a small pile in the sink, and burned everything. He watched the flames consume the words, and by chance they burned everything but his name and his date of birth. With a piece of wood, he rekindled the fire until all had turned to ash. His mother, alerted by the smell, rushed in:

"You've gone crazy! How will burning your diploma help anything? Now how are you going to apply for a teaching position? Three years gone up in smoke!"

Without a word, he collected the ashes, threw them into the trash, cleaned the sink, washed his hands, and then left. He was calm. He had no desire to speak about or to justify his action. What was the use of hanging on to a piece of paper that wasn't going to get him anywhere? His face remained inscrutable. His mother reminded him to pick up her medicine. The pharmacist would give it to him on credit, she said.

Later, he sat on a bench and stared at a trail of ants on

the ground. He asked a boy who sold loose cigarettes for one, lit it, and smoked slowly. The ants had deposited their loads and now headed back to where they had come from.

2.

His mind was made up: he would take over his father's cart. It was in bad shape. He would have to repair the wheels, replace a rotten plank, have the weighing scale re-calibrated, and get in touch with Bouchaïb, the fruit and vegetable supplier.

Where would he find the money? His mother had sold all her jewelry when his father became ill, and she had nothing left. Mohamed had heard about "microcredit." He looked into it, and was given a thick stack of forms to fill out. He was quickly discouraged by all the paperwork. He began to regret having burned his diploma.

Mohamed had won a trip to Mecca in a raffle at the Faculty of Arts and Letters, where he had studied. The one time he got lucky, he couldn't take advantage of it. What was he going to do with a plane ticket? He had no desire to go on a pilgrimage to Mecca, and, anyway, he didn't have the money to carry out the ritual. He wanted the airline to refund the cost of the ticket to him, but it refused. The only thing he could do was sell it to a pilgrim. He managed to get a third of the price, but still had to bribe the travel agent to change the name on the ticket. With the meager amount he had left, he repaired the cart and, finally, began to sell oranges and apples.

3.

Mohamed knew Bouchaïb was a crass and a very dishonest man. His father had often told him this. The man immediately claimed that Mohamed's father owed him money and hadn't paid his last two bills. How could Mohamed verify this? He had to come to terms with this guy because Bouchaïb was the only one who sold on credit—charging a markup of 10 to 15 percent. Mohamed didn't argue and gave him a deposit for two crates of oranges and one of apples; he also asked for a few baskets of strawberries.

Bouchaïb took him aside and, in a hushed voice, asked after his younger sister. Mohamed answered that she was doing well and was getting ready for her college entrance exam.

"You know, your father had promised her to me. I want to get married, have a family.

"You and I could even become partners. You can't make

ends meet with the fruit cart. There's a lot of competition, and, also, to get the right spot you have to be on good terms with the police."

Mohamed looked at him, bowed his head, and left without saying anything.

He didn't really know where to set up his cart. Some vendors moved around; others found themselves strategic spots, usually near an intersection or at a traffic circle. He soon realized that the best places were already taken, and decided to keep moving and stopping from time to time. He loudly hawked his oranges and apples, but it was useless because of the sound of honking horns. Nobody could hear him. When Mohamed stopped for a moment next to a grocer's stand, the owner instantly chased him off, shouting: "Are you crazy? What's wrong with you? I bought my license and I pay taxes. How am I going to make a living if you plant yourself right in front of me? Go on, get lost!"

On his first day, Mohamed just wandered around, from one street to another. Even so, he managed to sell more than half his produce. He realized that he would need to wake up very early the next day if he wanted a good spot before all the others arrived.

At dinner that night, he looked at his young sister and imagined her in Bouchaïb's arms. He felt ashamed. A young and innocent girl in the hands of a brute. Never.

4.

After dinner, he told his mother that Bouchaïb had demanded money from him.

"Your father couldn't stand having debts; he paid them off as soon as he could.

"Bouchaïb is a crook. He doesn't have any proof. Just forget about it. Did you remember to get my medicine? I only have one pill left."

Mohamed took out a box full of books and laid them out in front of the house for sale. History books, paperback novels, and a leather-bound copy of *Moby Dick* in English; it was a prize he had won for finishing at the top of his English class during his senior year at high school. He sold three books, making just enough to buy the medicine. He kept *Moby Dick*, as nobody had wanted it. That night, he reread a few pages and realized his English was a little rusty. Before falling asleep, he thought about beautiful Zineb, whom he had loved for two years. But with no money, no work, and no home of his own, it was impossible to get married. He was unhappy. What could he promise her when he had nothing to offer? He decided he had more pressing priorities, and he felt that he would succeed if he tackled things one at a time. Zineb would wait for him.

5.

Zineb worked as a secretary at a doctor's office. She really loved Mohamed. Being an only daughter, she had suggested that they get married and live at her parents' place. But Mohamed was proud; it was unthinkable for him to depend on his wife and live with his in-laws.

Usually Mohamed and Zineb met at a café. They talked a lot, kidded around, and often burst into laughter. More than three months had passed since they had been able to be alone to make love. The last time, Zineb's cousin had lent them her small apartment while her roommate was traveling.

"Someday," said Zineb, "we will reach the end of this tunnel. I promise you. I know it. I can feel it. You'll have a good job. I'll stop working for this sleazy doctor, and we'll start a life. You'll see."

"Yes, someday, but you know I'll never get on one of those flimsy boats to become an illegal. I know your plan: Canada! Yes, we'll all go to Canada, and we'll also go to paradise. It's written somewhere. But, in the meantime, I have to feed a big family, take care of my mother, and fight to get a good spot for my cart."

Zineb took his hands and kissed them. He took hers and did the same.

6.

Mohamed woke up at six. He tried to make as little noise as possible, so as not to wake his brothers, with whom he shared a room. There was Nabile, twenty years old, an unlicensed tourist guide, who often had problems with the police. There was Nourredine, eighteen, a high school student, who worked in a bakery from Friday evening until Monday morning. And then there was Yassine, fifteen, intelligent, lazy, handsome, and spiritual. He promised his mother that he would become a millionaire and take her to visit the Pyramids.

Mohamed washed himself, swallowed a piece of bread, and took out his cart. On top, he placed the box that he had used for his books. At the corner of their narrow street, a police officer stopped him:

"This is your old man's cart. Where is he?"

"He's dead."

"And you're just taking over, as if nothing had happened?"

"What's the problem? Is it forbidden to make an honest living?"

"Don't be insolent! Your papers."

Mohamed gave the man all the papers he had on him.

"No insurance. Can you imagine? If you ran over a kid, who would pay? You?"

"Since when is it necessary to have insurance for a fruit cart? This is new."

The police officer took out a notebook and started writing something while watching Mohamed out of the corner of his eye. After a moment, he said:

"You're playing the fool. Pretending you don't understand."

"I'm not doing anything. You're the one who's doing everything you can to keep me from going to work."

"OK, you can go now, but think about the insurance. I'm telling you this for your own good."

Then, with both his hands, the police officer helped himself to oranges and apples. He bit into an apple, and said, with his mouth full:

"Move on now!"

7.

Mohamed found a good spot; it was still quite early. He put down the cart and waited. A car stopped; the driver lowered the window and ordered: "One kilo of each, and get me the good ones." The next customers were in less of a hurry; they got out of their cars, felt the fruits, asked for the price, bargained, and ended up buying a few oranges.

An hour later, another vendor arrived with a decorated cart and a better, more attractive selection, including some expensive and rare exotic fruits. He had his regular customers. With a look and a slight nod of his head, the man indicated that Mohamed should leave this spot. He obeyed without protesting. Once again he had to wander the streets. He thought he had a good morning all the same, and he decided to have more variety the next time.

By the end of the day, he had sold everything. He went back to Bouchaïb to refill his cart.

That evening, despite being tired, he went to see Zineb at her parents' place. They liked him. He told Zineb about his day and ate some crepes with her before heading home.

8.

In the meantime, a plainclothes police officer visited Mohamed's mother. He asked her some questions about Mohamed and wanted to know why he didn't see the unemployed graduates' group anymore. The poor woman answered as well as she could, with hesitation and apprehension. The police officer handed her a summons according to which her son was to report to the police department that same evening. She started to cry, knowing that the police never brought good news. She thought it best to tell the officer: "My son is not political." The police officer left without saying anything.

When she gave Mohamed the summons, he looked at it and then stuffed it into his pocket.

"I'll go in a little while. They're going to interrogate me. If I don't go, they'll come for me, which will be even worse."

"My son, this visit has raised my blood sugar. I can feel it; my mouth is dry, and I don't feel well."

"These people are paid to create problems for us. In all likelihood, that cop comes from a family as poor as ours. But, as you know, the poor don't like one another."

9.

At the police department, Mohamed waited on a bench for a long time. From time to time he got up and tried to find out why he had been called in. Everyone ignored him. He suspected the summons was intended simply to intimidate him. He had received a similar summons when he first joined the unemployed graduates' demonstrations. Beside him sat an old man who was clearly impoverished; he didn't say a word, and seemed about to fall asleep. What could one hold against this man, who was coughing and spitting and who would be better off in a hospital room? Mohamed moved away from him. He was afraid of catching tuberculosis.

There was also a woman wearing a *djellaba*; she smoked cigarette after cigarette and railed against life.

"I was happy in my village. My God, why did I marry that imbecile who has now abandoned me?"

She called Mohamed to witness:

"I'm a prostitute! I am not ashamed to say it. But someday all this will change, you'll see. I've always had this feeling. It can't go on . . ."

Around midnight, a man signaled for Mohamed to follow him.

Identity verification.

Classic interrogation.

The police officer found it intriguing that Mohamed was no longer in touch with his former fellow activists. He wanted to know if the Islamists had approached him.

"No, it was my father's death that turned my life upside down. I took over his cart, our only means of survival."

"Yes, I know. How is it going?"

"I've barely got started."

"You know, there are no miracles. There are those who manage and make quite a bit of money, and there are others, the chumps, the losers. It's up to you to choose."

It took Mohamed some time to understand the deal the police officer was offering him: become an informer and have a profitable spot or refuse to serve the police and say good-bye to his business.

"Think about it hard. Tomorrow, I'll meet you at the Independence traffic circle. Now go home."

Mohamed knew if he showed up the next day at the appointed place, he would have to accept the cop's proposition.

Early in the morning, he took his cart and headed toward a working-class neighborhood far from the famous traffic circle.

10.

His mother's diabetes was out of control. She needed to go back to the doctor and get a new prescription. Mohamed made some calculations. Not enough money to meet this unexpected expense. He decided to take her to the public hospital. His seventeen-year-old sister went with them. He left them at the entrance and started to sell his produce. He realized that the hospital entrance was an excellent spot. People visiting the hospital bought fruit for the patients. An hour later, two police officers, one of them a woman, appeared before him:

"Your papers."

He gave them his papers.

"This is not your neighborhood. What are you doing here?"

"I brought my mother to the hospital. She has high blood sugar."

"Bless you *child*! It's good that you brought her here, but you'll be even more blessed if you clear out. We won't make you pay a fine this time, but you've been warned. Don't ever come here again. Is that clear?"

"But this is how I earn my living."

"God's Earth is vast."

Mohamed would have liked to answer that God clearly does not like the poor and the Earth *is* vast, but only for those with means. Yet he told himself, "It isn't worth making things worse for me. They are capable of arresting me for atheism."

He was perhaps not an atheist, but since the Islamists were almost everywhere now, he had distanced himself from religion. His father used to say to him, "The believer is destined for sorrow. God tests him, so be patient, my son!"

11.

Just when Mohamed was about to leave, a car stopped in front of him. The man, who seemed to be in a rush, asked him to weigh all his fruit and put it all in a big basket that he was holding out. "I want to buy it all. Today is a day of celebration, my son just graduated from high school. Can you believe it? I am going to send him to America, yes sir, to America, because here you can study day and night and then there's no work, but when you have an American degree, they hire you right away. I am happy. He's my only son. My daughters don't count. I can't get them married, nobody wants them. . . . Well, hurry up, quick, quick! How much is it? Calculate quickly. If you want I can help you." He took out his cell phone and started calculating as Mohamed dictated the numbers. "Well, it comes to two hundred and fifty-three rials. Here, three one hundred bills. You deserve it. You are a good guy. It shows."

Mohamed started pushing his cart toward the wholesale market. He wasn't going to go to Bouchaïb anymore. He would pay cash.

12.

At the end of the afternoon, he put his cart away and went to wait for Zineb at the entrance to her office. Nearby he saw a large number of busy young people. He was stunned by how many ways these people had thought of to make a living: there were vendors of loose American cigarettes; there were people speed-washing cars; some were helping the elderly who have trouble getting around; there were also sellers of hand-drawn postcards and toys made of soda cans; others were selling maps, or photographs of Michael Jackson and Ben Harper. There were acrobats dressed in red, who were performing tricks; there were monkey and parrot trainers; there were vendors of pirated DVDs, with films for all tastes—Indian, the latest American, classic films, Egyptian, and French; there were also storytellers with microphones pinned to their jackets. . . . Only snake charmers, fortune-tellers, sorcerers, and other swindlers were missing.

Then, suddenly, there was panic. The street vendors all began running—security agents were chasing them. Violently, the police managed to catch two people—a parrot trainer and a DVD seller. Blows, insults. The parrot was screaming. The DVDs lay crushed on the ground.

Among them was the movie *Spartacus*, starring Kirk Douglas. All that remained of the DVD was its sleeve. The two vendors were thrown into a National Security van. Mohamed felt like screaming, but he thought about his mother, about his entire family. He swallowed his anger and told himself, "I have to see Zineb."

He was glad to see her. He told Zineb about his day and avoided talking, at first, about the police violence on the street vendors. He proposed going to have some fish in a popular restaurant at the harbor. Soon the two of them were laughing like children lost in the middle of a splendid meadow on a spring day. Later he said to her, "The police defeated Spartacus! He was crushed under the tires of the van."

13.

They returned home on foot. On the way, they saw some street kids making a fire to warm themselves. One of them asked for a cigarette. "I don't smoke," said Mohamed, "but take this and buy something to eat."

The National Security vans drove slowly alongside them. Prostitutes were being asked for their papers. Zineb noticed one of the girls slipping a big banknote into the pocket of one of the cops. It's routine. That's how things go.

They discussed their marriage again.

"We have to wait. I just started working. I've got to pull off something big first."

"What do you mean?"

"Don't worry, I'm not going to hold up anyone! But I'd really like to open a store at the market. I know one of our neighbors who's sick, and he owns a well-located store in the central market. It would be great if he let me take over the store. I could pay for it little by little. I've looked into it. His children don't want to continue the business. They are engineers and technicians, so they don't have job problems. This would be an ideal solution for me. My mother is going to speak to the man."

"You're right. But I'm tired of waiting. We need to have our own place, even if it's just a shack, a small hole in the wall, a shed . . ."

14.

At home, the old TV was showing a program celebrating the President's thirty-year reign over the Republic. The President appeared with his wife, who had gained a lot of weight. Both wore makeup, were well dressed—too well dressed, too tidy, with not a hair out of place, and smug, satisfied smiles. The camera followed them through their palace, through their immaculate gardens with perfectly manicured trees and automatic sprinklers to water the grass. The President's wife was saying, "My husband works so hard that I have to force him to rest a little. Thank God the country is doing well. The people are grateful, and they show us their support every day, because they realize the country is prosperous and moving forward!"

The President made a gesture with his hand, as though waving to a child.

These images were accompanied by some syrupy background music, which got on Mohamed's nerves. His mother was dozing. His brothers and sisters were getting ready for bed. Yassine showed Mohamed his report card. For every class it said more or less the same thing: "Intelligent boy, talented student, but lazy. Could do better." Yassine laughed and said, "I get bored in the class, and, in any case, what's the point of studying? You've seen it yourself—you studied like crazy, and then no job. Now you've taken up Dad's cart."

Mohamed tried to give his brother some hope, but it was difficult. There was too much injustice in the country, too much inequality and humiliation.

Yassine told him that while returning home from school, he saw a man being beaten by the police. The man was screaming, and people stopped, but no one intervened. "I recognized the man. He's the caretaker of that glass building. You know, the one on the other side of our neighborhood. The man was fired, but nobody knows why. Today he stole a hen. It was bizarre. The man was screaming, and so was the hen, because he wouldn't let go of it. He really got a beating."

15.

Early the next morning, Mohamed left to buy his fruit. He bought a larger variety this time. Coming out of the market, he met a former fellow activist, who had got a job in the town hall.

"I don't do anything at the town hall. I'm in an office with four other clerks.

"Some of them have files to work on, but I don't. I'm bored. Plus, I haven't been paid. It has been six months. I live on credit. I think they hired some university graduates just to make us shut up, when in fact they don't have any positions for us. And how about you?"

"As you can see."

They said good-bye and parted. Ten minutes later, as Mohamed was waiting at a red light, two police officers in plain clothes pulled him aside.

"What were you and your friend talking about?"

"Nothing."

The first slap took Mohamed by surprise. He screamed and got a punch in his stomach.

"Shut the fuck up. Come on, what's your friend's name?"

"I forgot his name."

Another slap. The passersby stopped. One of the police officers threatened them:

"Clear off! He's a thief. We're doing this to protect you all. Let us do our job."

Mohamed cried, "It's not true! I am not a thief!"

Seeing the crowd close in on them, one of the police officers knocked the cart over and left Mohamed with all his fruit on the ground.

The crowd comforted him; they helped him pick up the fruit, though most of the strawberries were crushed. Some of the people said,

"This is disgusting! How shameful! Attacking a poor street vendor . . ."

"They behave as if they were in mafia movies. These bastards all want their share!"

"This can't go on! One day or other, God will bring the truth to light."

"God's on the side of the rich!"

Arguments follow.

"Villain! Infidel! God is with everyone! God is everywhere."

The people decided to buy Mohamed's fruit out of solidarity. He gave away the strawberry baskets that weren't crushed.

Mohamed didn't feel like working anymore; he felt sick.

He returned home, put away the cart, and, since his brothers were not home, he decided to take the opportunity to sleep and recuperate a little.

He had a dream. His father, dressed all in white, was beckoning to Mohamed to join him. He was saying something, but Mohamed couldn't hear him. He had no desire to join the deceased. Suddenly, his mother appeared and said, "Don't listen to what he's asking you to do. He is with God, perhaps in heaven."

In the morning, Mohamed woke, disturbed; the dream had been so powerfully real.

16.

It was high time that Mohamed and Zineb had cell phones. He bought two used phones in the central market. The phones were simple. No monthly charge, just a rechargeable SIM card, which allowed them to receive calls even when the credit was used up.

Mohamed also decided to improve his fruit cart. On one side, he set up a manual juice press to make orange juice. On the other side, he arranged the slightly better selection of fruit in a more appealing way. He also attached a board to show the prices. And, to make it look pretty, he hung a picture of the singer Oum Kalthoum. He even bought a flyswatter.

Mohamed seemed destined to become a wandering street vendor, since those who collaborated with the police took all the good spots. But this morning he decided to return to the neighborhood by the hospital, where business was good.

Soon two police officers arrived and started circling him.

"Oum Kalthoum! You like her voice? We do, too. But why have you hung the picture of an old singer who died a long time ago and not one of our beloved President? May God grant him a long life and prosperity!"

"I hadn't thought about it. If you want, I can remove the singer's picture."

"No, keep it, but hang a nice picture of our dear President above it, and one that's bigger than Oum Kaultoum's. OK?"

"OK."

The officers left. Mohamed was covered in cold sweat. He'd had enough of this almost daily harassment. He called Zineb and told her about the incident.

"They want you to give in. These people are rotten. Corrupt to the bone. I admire you for standing up to them."

"Do I have a choice?"

"So, shall we see each other this evening?"

"Yes, see you in the evening."

He found an old newspaper with a full-page picture of the President and tried to hang it on his cart. But each time he tried, the page kept falling. So he folded it up and put it under one of the crates. He would bring it out if they asked him again for a picture of the President.

17.

While Mohamed waited for customers on a busy street, a newspaper vendor stopped and handed him an Arabic newspaper. On the front page was written: "Scandal: An MP from the majority party extorted money from unem-

ployed graduates by making them fill out forms to emigrate to Canada. Five hundred rials per file and 252 victims. He has not been charged."

Mohamed knew about this swindle, and he would have
become a victim of it—if he had ever managed to save the
required amount for the "file fee."

The newspaper vendor said to him:

"You see, we can write about everything, denounce everything, but it doesn't change anything. The bastard is
still an MP. He raked in a huge amount of money, but the
authorities didn't take any action against him."

"You know, it wouldn't surprise me if one day one of
those victims slit his throat. After all, you can always take
justice into your own hands."

A sudden commotion.

Mohamed guessed that the police were making a
roundup; he quickly pushed his cart into a narrow alley-
way to hide. Some cats were fighting by an overturned
trash can; children played with plastic pistols.

He took a deep breath, crouched down, and held
his head in his hands; he felt like throwing everything
away and being done for good. But then he thought
of his mother, saw Zineb's face, his brothers, his sisters. . . . He got up and headed back toward the main
street.

18.

Mohamed had been working for more than a month despite the countless obstacles he encountered. This morning, for some reason, he had a bad feeling. As he was getting his cart out, one of the wheels fell off. He didn't know whether it was an accident or the result of sabotage. He had had problems with some of his neighbors who disapproved of his criticizing the regime. One day, the husband next door had said:

"If you continue speaking against the government, you're going to bring trouble on all of us. Why do you have to run everything down? Do you want everyone to be rich? You're a communist, aren't you? You'd better calm yourself, because, in this country, when the police arrest people you never know what shape they'll be in when they're returned."

"See, you too are criticizing the government."

"No, I'm only stating facts. I'm happy. Life is good."

Then he started shouting at the top of his lungs, "Long live the President! Long live the First Lady!"

Mohamed got down to repairing the wheel. Children stood around him, wanting to help. The cart was soon working again, and he left.

At the first intersection, a police officer stopped him.

"Where are you off to like this?"

"I'm going to work."

"Your work permit?"

"You know very well it doesn't exist."

"Yes, I know. But it can exist in other forms."

Mohamed pretended not to understand.

The police officer said:

"Too bad for you. This may cost you a lot more. See you later."

Mohamed left without turning around. He ran into a funeral procession. There were a lot of people, and, strangely, some of them were carrying the national flag.

Mohamed asked who was being buried:

"A poor guy, like you and me. No one knows exactly how he died. He was arrested last week for something to do with the Internet. Yesterday, his parents found his body dumped in front of their door."

"Killed by the police?"

"Clearly, but there's no proof," the man said in a low voice. "He was a great guy. He worked in a café, and in the evening, he played on the Internet."

Mohamed followed the procession while pushing his cart. He noticed that police officers in plainclothes were taking pictures.

After the burial, he left for the wholesale market.

19.

It was violent. He didn't even have time to get up. Two uniformed police officers, one of them a woman, threw him to the ground and seized the cart:

"Confiscated!"

"That's right, you have no right to sell illegally. You have no work permit, no license, and you don't pay taxes. You're stealing from the state. So it's over. Your cart is confiscated."

The female officer said:

"Now get lost. You'll get a summons to appear in court. Get the hell out of here!"

Mohamed remained on the ground, because the other officer was still kicking him.

Passersby stopped to watch. Some of them protested. The police threatened them. A jeep arrived, and an officer got out. After the police explained the situation, he got back into the jeep and disappeared.

Then a police van arrived. Other police officers got out and gathered the fruit that had fallen off the cart. One of them even bit into an apple he picked up.

Mohamed, powerless, said nothing, and then he cleared out.

He wandered through the streets, stunned by what

had just happened and incapable of thought. Without his realizing it, his steps carried him toward the town hall. He asked to speak to the mayor. The man at the front desk made quick circles at his temple with his index finger to indicate Mohamed was crazy:

"You think you can see the mayor just like that?"

"Why not? I need to speak to him."

"Who do you think you are to talk to him? Are you rich? Are you important? Now, get out of here and let me drink my tea in peace." Mohamed insisted:

"Perhaps the deputy mayor . . ."

"They're all out. The governor is opening a new mosque."

"And tomorrow?"

"Let me give you some advice. Drop it."

"All right, but before I go, let me tell you why I want to speak to the mayor."

"Why?"

"The police confiscated the one thing I need to make a living, the cart I use to sell fruit. It's my livelihood."

"And you think the mayor will overrule the police for the sake of your beautiful eyes?"

"For the sake of justice."

"Well, aren't you special! Where did you come from?"

Lowering his voice a little, the man asked:

"Where have you seen justice done in this country?"

Then he stepped out for a moment and returned armed with a club.

"Now, get lost! Or else, I'll break your pretty face."

Mohamed didn't insist anymore.

20.

That evening, he saw Zineb, who suggested that she go with him to the town hall. Also, she had another idea:

"And what if we went directly to the chief of police?"

"Why not?"

They went to the police headquarters.

None of the officers knew about Mohamed's situation. Zineb spoke first:

"Well, in that case we are going to press charges for theft!"

"You're going to file a charge against the police? Where do think you are, in Sweden?" the officer asked with a wicked smile.

"We just want our cart back."

"I understand you. Give me your ID cards so that I can make photocopies, and I'll contact you if there's any news."

Zineb didn't trust him; she refused, pulled Mohamed by his arm, and they left.

They walked through the streets for a long time, holding hands, and, at times, with their arms around each other's waist.

A car pulled up beside them.

Plainclothes police officers said:

"Your papers."

"But you're not married. It's illegal to walk in deserted streets at this time of the night."

Zineb used her charm and begged the officer not to report them.

"My father's very violent. Please, let us go. We'll go home. We weren't doing anything wrong."

"OK, get going. You're off the hook this time."

They both went straight home.

Mohamed had a very restless night; he hadn't told his mother about what happened. Stress made her blood sugar rise, his father had said.

21.

Early the next morning, Mohamed washed himself, and then, for the first time since his father's death, he decided to pray. He changed into clothes that were all white. His mother was asleep; without waking her, he kissed her forehead. He glanced at his sleeping brothers and sisters. Then he ran out of the house. He borrowed his brother's old motorbike, stopped at a gas station and filled a plastic water bottle with gasoline. He put the bottle in a small bag and headed toward the town hall.

Once there, he asked to see an official.

No one wanted to see him.

He returned to the place where the two police officers had confiscated his cart.

They were there again, and the cart was in a corner. Empty.

Mohamed went up to them and asked to have his cart back.

The male officer slapped him hard and shouted:

"Look, you dirty rat; get lost before I beat the shit out of you!"

Mohamed tried to defend himself. This time the female officer took her turn slapping him and spitting on his face. She shouted:

"You creep, you're spoiling our breakfast! You have no manners. You're a nobody . . ."

Mohamed lay prostrate. He didn't speak anymore, didn't move anymore; his face was immobile, his eyes were red, his jaws clenched. Something inside him was about to explode. He stayed in this position for two or three minutes—to him, it felt like an eternity.

The male officer said:

"Go on, get out of here. Your cart, you'll never see it again. It's all over. You've shown us no respect. And, for this, you pay a price in our beloved country."

Mohamed's mouth was dry, his saliva bitter. It was hard for him to breathe. He said to himself, "If I had a gun, I would empty it into these bastards. I don't have a gun, but I still have my body, my life, my wasted life. This is my weapon."

22.

Mohamed got to his feet and backed away from them. He started up the motorbike and headed back toward the town hall.

He locked his bike to a pole when he arrived and again asked to speak to the mayor or one of his deputies. The man at the front desk was even more furious than he had been the day before. Back outside, Mohamed thought about the bottle of gasoline in the small bag, adjusted his white clothes, and walked around the square. No one noticed him.

It was a sunny December morning. The seventeenth of December. A confused jumble of images rushed through his mind: His mother in bed, his father in his coffin, himself at the Faculty of Arts and Letters, Zineb smiling, Zineb angry, Zineb begging him not to do anything; his mother getting out of bed and calling for him; the face of the woman who had slapped him earlier, who slapped him again; his body bent forward as though he were offering himself to an executioner; the blue sky; a huge tree sheltering him; himself in Zineb's arms under the tree; himself as a child, running so as not to be late for school; his French teacher praising him; himself taking his college exams, showing his diploma to his parents; the diploma pinned to a sign beside the word *unemployed*; his diploma burning in the sink at his place; his father's burial again; screams; birds; the President and his wife wearing huge black sunglasses; the woman who had slapped him; the other who had insulted him . . . a procession of sparrows crossing the sky; *Spartacus*; a public faucet; his mother and his two sisters standing in line to get water; the police brutalizing him again; insults, blows, insults, blows . . .

One last time, Mohamed asked to see the mayor. Refusals and insults. The man at the front desk pushed him with his club and he fell to the ground. Mohamed rose in silence and went to stand in front of the town hall's main entrance. He took the bottle of gasoline from the bag, poured it over himself, from head to toe, until the bottle was empty. Then he lit his Bic lighter, looked for a moment into its flame, and drew it toward his clothes.

The fire ignited instantly. Within moments, the crowd ran toward him. The front-desk clerk screamed. He tried to put out the fire with his jacket, but Mohamed had transformed into a torch. By the time an ambulance arrived, the fire was out, but Mohamed had lost all human resemblance. He was entirely black, like a grilled lamb.

The front-desk clerk was crying, "It's all my fault. I should have helped him."

23.

Mohamed is in the hospital. His entire body is wrapped in bandages. Like a shroud. He is in a coma. A commotion in the hallways. Doctors in white coats and nurses race down the hallway that leads to Mohamed's room. The President has come; the President has just inquired about Mohamed's fate. The President is not happy. He hears about the mayor who refused to see Mohamed. He orders him fired. The President is angry. He finds out that the international press is covering the story.

A horde of doctors follows the President into the hospital room.

Obscene and ridiculous displays.

The entire country is in revolt. With her hair tied back, Zineb is leading a demonstration. Her fist raised, she's shouting and screaming.

Mohamed dies on January 4, 2011.

There are demonstrations everywhere. Everyone is shouting: "We are all Mohameds."

The President leaves the country like a thief. His plane disappears into the starry night.

24.

More demonstrations in the country.

Photographs of Mohamed are everywhere. A victim and a symbol. The international media rush to the country to interview his family.

Even a film producer comes to see them. He hands an envelope to the crying mother and says:

"Please accept this help. It's not much. Such is fate, cruel and unjust."

Then he bends down and whispers into the weeping woman's ear:

"It's important that you don't speak to anyone else. Don't give any interviews to journalists. I am going to help you. I will tell Mohamed's story. The entire world should know what happened. Mohamed is a hero, a victim, and a martyr. Do we agree? You will not speak with anyone else but me. I have to go now, but if you need anything at all, here's my card, and here's a cell phone so you can call me."

The mother didn't understand anything this person said. But her two daughters understood very well: "This guy wants to buy our brother's death and profit from it! How horrible! What an utter nightmare!" Mohamed's story doesn't belong to anyone. It's the story of a simple man, like millions of others, who, from being crushed, humiliated, and denied in life, became the spark that set the world ablaze. No one can ever steal his death.